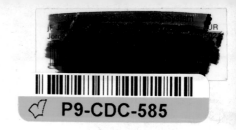

HIS
OWN
WHERE

DEDICATED TO THE LIVING

Buddy and Angela
Julius
Jodi
David and Barbara

HIS
OWN
WHERE

June Jordan

THOMAS Y. CROWELL COMPANY New York

L.C. Card 71-146283
ISBN 0-690-38133-6

2   3   4   5   6   7   8   9   10

the first page

You be different from the dead. All them tomb-
stones tearing up the ground, look like a little city,
like a small Manhattan, not exactly. Here is not
the same.

Here, you be bigger than the buildings, bigger
than the little city. You be really different from
the rest, the resting other ones.

Moved in his arms, she make him feel like smiling. Him, his head an Afro-bush spread free beside
the stones, headstones thinning in the heavy air.
Him, a ready father, public lover, privately at last
alone with her, with Angela, a half an hour walk
from the hallway where they start out to hold
themselves together in the noisy darkness, kissing,
kissed him, kissed her, kissing.

Cemetery let them lie there belly close, their
shoulders now undressed down to the color of
the heat they feel, in lying close, their legs a strong
disturbing of the dust. His own where, own place
for loving made for making love, the cemetery
where nobody guard the dead.

one

First time they come, he simply say, "Come on."
He tell her they are going not too far away. She go
along not worrying about the heelstrap pinching
at her skin, but worrying about the conversation.
Long walks take some talking. Otherwise it be
embarrassing just side by side embarrassing.

Buddy stay quiet, walking pretty fast, but every
step right next to her. They trip together like a
natural sliding down the street.

Block after block after block begin to bother
her. Nothing familiar is left. The neighborhood is
changing. Strangers watch them from the windows.

Angela looking at Buddy, look at his shoes and
wish for summertime and beaches when his body,
ankle, toes will shock the ocean, yelling loud and
laughing hard and wasting no sand.

Buddy think about time and the slowspeed of

her eyes that leave him hungry, nervous, big and quick. Slide by the closedup drugstore, cross under the train, run the redlight, circle past two women leaning on two wire carts, and reach the avenue of showrooms. Green, blue, yellow, orange cars driving through, cars at the curb, cars behind the glass, cars where houses used to stand, cars where people standing now, and tree to tree electric lights.

"Play the radio?"

Buddy turn it with his thumb. The plastic handle strings around his wrist.

> No moon no more
> No moon no more
> I want to see what I seen before.

> Please no surprise
> Please no surprise
> I just want to see your lovin eyes.

Holding her hand in his is large and hers almost loose inside it. She feel visitor-stiff, but the music make a difference, and his hand.

Cars make Buddy mad. Right now his father lying in the hospital from what they call A Accident. And was no accident about it, Buddy realize. The street set up that way so cars can clip the people easy kill them even. Easy.

"What you say?," she ask him.

"Damn," he answer her. "Another one. Another corner. Street-crossing-time again."

"You crazy, Buddy? What you mean?"

"I hate them. Corners. They really be a dumb way try to split the people from the cars. Don't even work. Look how a car come up and almost kill my father, minding his own business, on the corner. Corners good for nothing." Buddy frown so bad that Angela start laughing. Buddy swing around her waist.

"Show you what I mean."

He jump back behind her. Walk forward like a flatfoot counting steps: Left-foot-right-foot-left-foot-one-two.

"Here come the corner!"

Down. Buddy buckle at the knee for *down.* When he really reach the corner then he drop to one knee. Seem like a commando on the corner. Wild looking left then right. Arms like a rifle in rotation: Covering the danger east and west. Buddy standing on his two feet urgent. Put his face an inch from her: "Watch now. Here. It's here." He roll the radio dial to loud yell over it. "Not clear! Not clear at the crossing. On your mark" (whispering in her ear), "get set." Buddy stop. "Green. Where's the green? You seen it, Angela?" He fold his arms and spread his legs and hold everything right there. "Well my Lookout Man is out to lunch." Buddy sitting on the curb, to wait.

Angela feel a question, but the radio so loud she would have to scream. With him, she rather not be screaming.

Angela not laughing and no smile. Buddy sitting on the curb and she beside him, so he roll the dial to soft.

"You see them signs. The curb-your-dog signs. But the people be like slaves. Don't need no signs. Just do it. Curb-the-People. Step right up, then down, then up. Then out. Into it. Into the traffic, baby. You be crucify like Jesus at the crossing. Traffic like a 4-way nail the joker on his feet. It be strictly D.O.A. for corners. Danger on Arrival. D.O.A. Even dogs can smell that danger, smell it just as good as looking at the lights. You tired?"

"No," She is. But nothing they can do about that. No bench. No sidewalk, walkway tables, benches. Only fences fixed outfront.

"Buddy, this no place to stop."

Rises from the curb, his arm around her, moving on together, slower walking easy on the edge. The sidewalk is a concrete edge.

The lined-up traffic multiplies. The fenders blur. Windshield swiping windshield chrome and auto-colors. Hold her close, his side comes long and close beside her.

At the intersection they will cross together. Intersection circus stunt for everyday.

"Angela, look out."

She hear his shaking inner sound. She listen to him. Coordination is together trial.

Matched to her to him out in the middle of the mess machinery. He be strong enough and she be fast enough to swerve it safely through, across, around, ahead. Landed on the other edge, the sidewalk opposite. She smell intoxicating leather jacket, how he wears it, how he smells to her.

He slowly flaming from the small size of her neck, its naked expectation.
"Buddy, this is a cemetery. Let's go back."
"No. Let's go on."
"I don't like it here."
"Why not?"
"You know why."
"Angela, where can we go beside the cemetery. What else is there?"
"We can go home."
"Home." The idea, the memories, the fact of home straightens him away from her, from what she probably mean.
"Just trust me five more minutes. Trust me." They step ahead, single file. She following him. He leading them, both of them. Trees like a skinny curtain start appearing. What they can see are cemetery furnishings. Somebody leave a potted plant. The flabby petals from the $4.95 racketeer store close to the scene of the absolutely dead.

They notice the one-by-one increasing trees. She watch Buddy how he walk ahead of her, how he seems a bit ahead of her. They come to a silent place. The only sounds, the engine highway sounds.

They climb up sidesoil to a fence that stretches high above their heads and out beyond armstretching.

Angela be blinded by the light wiggles blinding in the silent waterfills her eyes. They say nothing, just look and feel full. It be like a big open box, sides of sloping stone, moss covered rainy dark and, behind them, a little to the left, there be a small brick tower room, a locked-up house where no one ever live.

Buddy say, "This is the reservoir." Angela be thinking *water* and, over by the furthest rim of it, they see the roof of streets and houses that they know. Nobody close to them. Buddy and Angela begin to make believe about the house next to the reservoir. They see how they would open it up, how they would live inside, what they would do with only the birds, the water and the skylight fallen blinding into it.

"What they saving the water for? Who suppose to use it."

"Saving it for birds. This a bathroom for the birds."

They laugh about the pretty water bathroom for the birds.

"Be nice if we can swim here."

"They not hardly let you swim in it. Unless you be a bird."

Go over to the doorsill of the house, sit down for talking.

"Why you bring me here?"

"You don't like it?"

"So quiet. I don't know."

"How come you always want some sound?"

"Real quiet bother me. But then again, when I go to like the supermarket they be playing loony tunes and you be looking at a can of soup, or pork chops, but you have to hear dah-dah-blah-blah and violins and mustard and potatoes dah-dah-blah-blah-violins, it can make you feel really weird."

"So what you want to hear with mustard and potatoes?"

"Well, could be somebody like that kind of music, but I don't. I rather be hearing other things. Like if you play the radio and we decide what we want to hear I mean at this very moment."

"What you want?"

"You talk to me, Buddy. Tell me what you thinking."

They have to leave soon. Reservoir growing dim. They have to walk back.

"What you doing tonight?"

"Study, can you stop by after you see your father?"

"I don't know. Might be really too late."

"Is he better?"

"No. My relatives rap strong about insurance and inheritance. I say he be dying, but not dead. And at the hospital they be fooling with him. Half the time I go, can't see him. They exploring this or that, testing him for what not. The other half, he be sleeping, from the pills they give him. The dude that knock him down, you know that dumbhead driver? Last week he actually come by, call himself paying some respects. I tell him that respect don't make him better, but I say well let him come. Don't make no difference. My father dying lonely and I figure that respect don't hurt a lonely man."

Call it accidental but to him, to Buddy, was no accident. Things set up like that. You cross the street you taking chances. Odds against you. Knock his father down, down from the sidewalk stop, down from the curb, down bleeding bad, ribs crushed. The lungs be puncture, and his father living slow inside a tent.

two

The hospital seem nice. Nothing too loud or filthy, beds adjustable, regular food. Different people, men and women, asking how you are, how you feel. Friends drop around. Privacy. Whole attitude all allright. You suppose to heal, be well, stay well in the hospital.

Don't let no rumbly trucks rock through the streets. Floors be clean enough to eat on. Buddy sure the whole city should be like a hospital and everybody taking turns to heal the people. People turning doctor, patient, nurse. Whole city asking asking everybody how you are, how you feel, what can I do for you, how can I help.

Fantastic if the city turn into a hospital the city fill with a million people asking a million other people how you feeling, how's everything, what you need. Dig, policeman move up to this Momma, ask her do she sleep well.

She say no. Explaining how the heat turn off at midnight. Policeman make a note. Act like a nurse.

That was how he meet her, Angela. Inside the hospital. Father dying in a semiprivate room more private than the room he share so many years ago, with Buddy's mother. Semiprivate room for dying seem all right. Who want to be alone, completely. Seem all right for living too; a semiprivate room for keep alive. Buddy by the bed, sitting still. His mind remembering home.

Brownstone and cigar smoke. Women pocketbooks and peppermint. Shined shoes. His father sharpening the Sunday razor slap the leather slap the blade to silver sharp. In the bureau drawer blue enamel cufflinks, brassy bullets from the war. Few photographs. His mother prim-sarcastic posing straight ahead. Old box of contraceptives. Blow them up. Bounceback old-timer tricks from when.

When his mother and his father in the double-softbed underneath the walnut crucifix cost not so much as you might think. It be so heavy hanging there above the doubledecker pillows too clean for anybody use them. But they use them when they use to be asleep around the morning after Buddy father do his downtown nightwatch. And before when Buddy mother leave without him, Buddy. Disappear his father say without no reason.

But Buddy remember how his mother use to stay gaze on the ground around the neighborhood. She brokenhearted in the brokenland of Brooklyn small-scale brokenland. She cry the day they rip one tree right out the concrete ground in front of the dining-room windows. Tree already attacked by lightning on a rainy afternoon when Buddy watch the men their caps firm to the eyebrows walking to the corners, carrying a paper bag of lunch. And when he watch the women breasted motherly and crooked walking with a Horn and Hardart/Bargaintown/Macy's Christmas shopping bag. The dining room, where she cry that day, on other days unusual with celery and olives.

Sweet port wine and soda, flower wineglasses, crochet lacy tablecloth, and two red candles definitely lit. The greens and ham the rice and peas and cheese and crackers and tomato juice standing in small glasses on small glassy plates. The perspiration smell of toilet water. Buddy, helping carve, he feel the swarm of aunts and uncles cousins. Feel them sweaty near, amazing and predictable. And rhinestones and the wellmade grayplaid special suit. The hugging and the jokes. The sudden ashtrays and his mother in a brandnew apron serving. Serving and remote. Retreating to the kitchen sink excuse from laughter where the family relax drink rum to celebrate another year survival. His mother serving her way out of the loosely loving festival of food and thankyou to the Lord.

His father when he help to dry the dishes silverware pots cup and saucers try to bring her into the ordinary comfort of his arms and she collapse in them unhappy. "We need another cabinet," she tell his father. She continuous in putaway and polish: sort and starch. "This is our own house," she would repeat. "We sacrifice, we save and borrow for this house. At least it is our own. Or will be." And then she say, "I know it is not beautiful, but it is clean."

She leave it, finally. When she leave them then his father turn to him, to Buddy and the house. The house become a house of men strip to the basic structure truth of it, the four rooms gradual like one that spreads around the actions of a day. His mother hungering for order among things themselves, for space she could admire, simply hungering and gone. Where did she go, and Buddy wondering about this last disorder she did not repair. This disordering of life of marriage of her motherhood. Strange lovely woman warm and hungering and gone.

Buddy father clean the house down to the linoleum. Remove the moldings. Take away the window drapes and teach him, Buddy, how to calculate essentials how to calculate one table and two chairs, four plates, two mugs. Together they build shelves and stain them. Throw out the cabinets and bureaus opening and closing like a bank. His father teach him hammering and saws and measuring and workshop science. House be like a workshop where men live creating how they live. Throw out the lamps and build lights into the ceiling. Indirect direct white/lavender. Buddy working with wires and pliers rush from school to work beside his father on the house.

On duty in the night his father dream and draw the next plan for the next day, working the house into a dream they can manage with their hands. Years like this working on the way they live with open shelves and changing furniture from store to slowly made in wood they pick up awkward.

Buddy see him sleeping and unconscious. Bandages a brace a cast a bruise black swollen on the brown skin of his face. His father face asleep, unshaven. Thick lips promising to speak to smile again. Eyes closed. No intimation of their waking focus gentle calculating inches and diameter or grain. A short man, Buddy's father, short and powerful and maybe handsome. Buddy not sure what handsome mean, in general, but to him, to Buddy, this man, his father, is a lonely, handsome man, powerful and short.

three

From the other side of the other bed the nurse was speaking to him, that longago first time.

"Don't you have no mother, boy?"

Buddy stare back sullen.

"You don't have to answer me. A woman my age know who has a mother and who don't. You don't. You don't have no mother. Night after night, from afternoon you come sit by your father. Very nice, and what you should be doing. But how old you getting to be and what they call you?" Buddy stir himself, feeling most of all surprise. The woman talk like a knife try to butter but cuts the bread.

"Sixteen."

"I know you was sixteen. Or seventeen. Who's taking care of you and what's you name?"

"Buddy. Buddy Rivers."

"Well, that's all right too, but who is taking care of you, when you leave the hospital, Buddy Rivers?"

"Everything's okay. We got things under control."

"That's how all you young people answer me. Everything is mind your own business, am I right?"

Buddy be annoy by now. The woman is a private nurse for the patient in the next bed. Be bad to make an enemy have to see an enemy in the same room where his father dying. And her question bother him. His relatives ask the same thing and discuss where he should move. Assume that he should move out of the house he and his father put together like their lives until now. Move! He will not move among the doilies, wallpaper, headboard beds, and extra extra chairs that scatter through the houses of his relatives. The gold-thread sofabeds. The monstrous glossy large television console. The wobbling bright installment furniture and Woolworth bric-a-brac that make it dangerous to stretch your legs straight out or swing your arms around. He will not move. It is a home they made. Not very clean in the usual way. But beautiful and full of what they absolutely need for everyday. Full and free from stuff just lying and lying around.

"I'm sure your father would expect you to show respect when people speak to you," the nurse was saying. That was the whole nagging way she came on on the first night that she talk to him, to Buddy.

Buddy could never get over this difference between women and their daughters. Like this nurse, this obnoxious, nosy woman who spoke to him like that when they were strangers, she was the mother of his Angela. She was the mother of the girl Buddy felt guilty to be so aware of there right where his father lay, his face asleep, his life dying. But he was. He was even waiting for her. Weeks before they even spoke, he would feel himself waiting for the girl whose name he didn't know.

Every evening around eight, just before the end of visiting hours, she would come and get her orders from headquarters. Her mother jangling with coins and keys and inquiries and orders: who ate what for dinner, who was where, and so forth. Angela was pretty. And she was pretty cool. He could tell she was embarrass by his witness to the nightly scene. But she keep cool. Keep her voice down low, releasing monosyllables as brief as possible:

"Yes. Okay. You said that. I won't. I did it."

She was pretty. And he like the coolness. The splash tongue of her mother inhibit both of them. Neither said hello.

Buddy always remember how the woman sizzle with suspicion even before Angela and him really start to talking with each other.

Then one time when Angela come by, wearing jeans and looking comfortable, her mother run through a tirade so tough that Buddy try to help out Angela and introduce himself and walk her home. The tirade start because of the bluejeans:

"Angela! Did you forget something?"

"Don't think so."

"Did you forget you were coming here to see me in the hospital?"

"What's the matter?"

"What's the matter? You see how you dress and you askin me what is the matter. Are you a hippy? You think a hospital is a hippy hangout? This is a hospital and I am a professional woman. And I am your mother. Look at you."

Angela try to walk out. The woman seize Angela by the arm and snarl upclose.

"You wait right there. I'm not finish talking to you. Do you hear me?"

Buddy want to interfere.

"And you, Mr. Rivers, you can sit right down again. What you standing for?"

"I think you should let go of Angela."

"Angela, you saying. Angela. What other names you call each other, I would like to know. You pretending not to know each other all this time and what's the truth behind it?"

"I hear you call her Angela, that's all," Buddy say, still standing.

Angela be trembling furious. The woman whirl and scream at her. "On top of everything, you better not let me see you evil lip."

"I be as evil as I want to be."

"All right. You said it."

"I say what? Let me go, Ma."

The woman smack Angela in the face.

"You finish, Ma? You finish now?"

"No. I'm not finish. I'm just starting with you. Come back here."

Angela break through the doorway, knowing her mother probably will not leave the patient by himself to follow her. Buddy follow Angela.

"What you want?" Angela be crying but no streaming tears.

"Let me walk you home." Buddy catch up to her, walking along, worrying about her face. Thinking, feeling about Angela, he almost forget his father.

On the street they walk separated.

"Why the two of you go on like that?"

Angela feel stung: "the two of you." She like the solid look of Buddy dark out the corner of her eyes upon her mother every night. Him, Buddy sitting there sly don't miss a minute of the interaction. Still he say, "the two of you." What did he mean? They walk separated. She not answering the question, hurt.

Streets turning off except for candystores, and liquor stores and iron grates dull interlocking over glass. Except for the bars the people party high, knees and feet poke rapid sharp toward an indoor kitchen, bedroom. People hurry calmly from the nighttime start to glittering like oil.

"My mother picking on me, picking, picking on me. I wish she would just kick me out."

"You must be the oldest."

"I am. Three brothers younger than me, and then a baby sister. My mother work and scream. My daddy work and both of them work nights. The problem is they think I'm working nighttime too— They think I'm maybe running the streets."

"What your father do?"

"Driving a cab. So I take care of all the cooking. Baby-sit. But I try to study anyhow."

"Where you go to school?"

"Lane."

"Didn't know people studying at Lane. Thought you people just fight and then just fight some more."

"Oh, come on! Only thing we did was try to raise the flag of liberation. Now you know how folks react to liberation. But I been hearing about you. At Boys' High. I even know your name."

She don't tell him how she hear how he suppose to be so fine and really B A D and have the teachers shook and shaking. Buddy have a lot of friends hanging out with him at school. They stick together pretty tight, and he have a reputation everybody say the same about him so she hear things all the time.

When they reach her building Buddy see chalk scribbling on the granite and the outside stairs curve interesting worn.

Angela ask him inside.

Two of her brothers, Ronald, three, and Edwin, eleven, in front of the TV, wearing undershirts and

BVDs. The third brother, eight-year-old Tyrone wearing the same, in the bathroom floating a TV dinner tray in the bathtub. Angela take Buddy to her room where the baby, Debby, is sleeping. A doll carriage holding Debby asleep. Angela have a cot and ironing on top of it, she have to iron. Over by the radiator a scratch formica table and chair Angela use for studying. An overhead three-socket fixture, one bulb screw into it. Long nails in the wall hold clothing, hangers, dresses, skirts and jackets hung on them.

Buddy feel depression in the clutter-stricken room. Feel like a carpenter hands tied. Want to toss out everything and start the room from scratch. Keep it bare enough so Angela feel free.

"Your parents think you pretty wild." Buddy not quite leaning on the edge of the table desk. "Are you?"

Angela answer, giggling. "You believe it. After I cook dinner, feed my baby sister, I drag over hear my mother, come back, wash or iron, study, worry about my father when he come home will he be shaking me awake and want to carry on, complain, and like that, I am pretty wild. Just like my mother say, a freak for parties."

Buddy dig on the fantastic stack of 45's piling from the floor. "Don't you have no phonograph?"

Angela say no and she explain why she don't play her records in the parlor where her father turn hysterical and call the music sinful. Call her when she dance and sing "a whore."

Buddy like this girl, this Angela. He hate the room

she have. Make even Angela seem clumsy. Make him feel himself like overgrown from Mars. He hate the whole apartment skimpy on the people-space. Rooms crush small by stuffed-up piece of furniture huge sofa and huge matching lamps huge things that squeeze the family mix into a quarrel just to move around a little. But all he say, that first night when he look at how she live at home is that he see her in the hospital, tomorrow.

four

His life form into habits following his love. Angela and the hospital and his father all roll into hours that he spend with them. Now every night he be walking Angela home from the hospital and then he go back there and stay there at the hospital watching his father/the body of his father on the hospital bed until they make him leave.

Sometimes Buddy wishing he could bring Angela to the house sanded and hammered into a home by him and his father. The house of things eliminated. The house made simple into home where Buddy waiting to know his father again alive in action taking a wall apart or building a low wall like a window ledge between two rooms.

Angela parents carry on so strict and wild that Buddy can only see her every day. Walking home. And for half a minute visits when her father may be sure to be out working. Or a few times managing the walk into the cemetery on a weekend afternoon. And one time at a party. And sometimes at the store.

Buddy and Angela keep track of daytime just by figuring out the last and then the next time they will come together for how long alone. They become the heated habit of each other.

five

Another evening and Angela mother rip into the love between them. Say she cannot sleep for worrying about her daughter and "that poor man, your father" and his son, Buddy.

Buddy ask the woman why she worrying and what about. The woman sob and shriek and curse at Angela and call her nogood lowdown. Angela feel humiliated and refuse to answer back.

Again her mother smack her in her face and Angela break away running. That night after Buddy walk Angela home he does not go back to see his father at the hospital. His head feel heavy and his feet.

Instead, Buddy slide into the darkness, thinking and feeling about Angela, and find himself walking to his father house. Buddy takes the sidewalk broom from inside and come out to the cold night, sweeping the stoop, the stairs, the yard, the sidewalk. Sweeping under the night. Ragged and shrill in the ragged shrubbery three or four male cats howl close to the female magnet listening calm.

Buddy consider bothering the cats but change his mind.

Back into the house, the workshop of his father and his life and wanders heavily and tall inside the easy space.

Saying her name, Angela. Pretending she is here to dance with him here where nothing but himself will move.

The phonograph lies low along one wall on a board shelf where the parts in factory packages remind him of the work to do the wires to organize attach. Work interrupted by the accident that snatch his father. Buddy start to fool with parts and try to concentrate on diagrams of wiring and speaker placement. But he be thinking Angela.

In the kitchen, absentminded opening a can of soup, stirring with a wooden spoon. Into the basement opening with a screwdriver a can of black lacquer paint, stirring with a wooden spatula. Back upstairs to relocate the (parts of the) phonograph packages. Buddy abandon the phonograph project. Next he remove a long piece of lumber from its wall hinge supports. Clean it, start to paint it.

Lacquer shining smoothly. Black black like a glisten polishing the lumber plank he handle easily. The black the lacquer black glistening lumber invitation to his touch and finger press he better not. Too soon to touch still wet. Too soon to touch like Angela. Too soon to really touch her.

six

When Angela father come home drunk that night the phone ring and he hear his wife telling him that Angela defy disgrace them in the hospital calling her a loudmouth woman.

Angela father smile at this but still his wife continue: "She left here with a boy. Were you there when they came home?"

"What boy?"

Angela mother explain how Angela run out on her because she wouldn't hardly leave the bedside of her patient. She describe how the boy, Buddy, follow after her, Angela, and how the boy, whose father be dying in the hospital bed, how the boy never come back to the bedside of his father, that night. Is he, the boy, in that house with Angela? What did the devil daughter do with the boy? That devil daughter can't be trust no way. She making it impossible for decent people try to earn a living to go out with easy mind and earn they bread.

Angela father say he will take care of it, find out what is going on behind they back. Hang up the phone. A spare, goodlooking man. Slip into the room where Angela in bed, turn a flashlight on her face.

"Angela, get up," he shout at her.

"Angela!"

Rubbing her eyes from sleep she see him stepping on the clothes she have iron and stack by her bed.

"Move, Daddy—"

That's as much as she can say. His fist come down her face, her cheek. She scream aloud. His knuckle slap her head around, and pound her punching through to ribs. Angela struggle her hand under the pillow where to protect herself she hide a kitchen knife not to be beaten like she is. Seize the handle, whip the knife into his view and tell him "Leave me alone."

"You little prostitute."

He kick the cot over and she fall to the floor face down and lose the knife. He leap beside her beating her across her back.

"You get out of this house, get out of this house, get out."

Angela pass out. Her father pause, then drop his arm and leave the room. After a while Angela come to. Her mouth taste ugly. She wince to move. She listen if she hear him near, awake. Hear nothing. Tears come from the pain of putting her coat around her. She struggle down into the street. It be almost morning. Angela staggering, bolt and collapse along the street toward Buddy house. Some men in a old Cadillac try to pick her up (thinking she drunk) until one of them come close enough to see her swollen face and bloody.

Angela use all her strength to ring the bell. Buddy look through the dining-room window where his mother watch the tree rip from the concrete and he see his girl fallen down small against the first floor window bars.

Angela. He bring her inside into the house the home of his life where he imagine her, but never, not this way, so fallen small she only seem a small girl. Buddy try to see how bad it is. He feel like vomiting. The loneliness is gone but in place of loneliness, this stranger Angela, so small.

Look at her, afraid. Wrap her warm and carry her to his father car. Drive to the hospital.

The attendant in the Emergency Room act very suspicious. "You beat up your girlfriend. Then you want us to patch her up for you, so you can beat her up some more."

He look at Angela.

"She just a baby. You should be ashame."

He look at Buddy.

"You just a kid yourself. What's her name?"

"Angela."

Man call the police.

Angela unconscious so she can't answer any of the questions that you have to if you want the hospital to treat you. Police come and question him, Buddy, and he tell them the street, house, and apartment of her parents. The police tell him stay there until they return.

Buddy leaning on the rear wall of the Emergency Room. His body tight, fearing for Angela untended as the time continues to count by. Aides have taken her away from the waiting-room area, put her on a rolling steel-strong stretcher, cover lightly by a single sheet. Buddy leaning tired and horrify at the back of the gigantic room. Rows of churchly hardback wooden pews. Fat women slow tears from they eyes, they waiting. Girls, with babies on they knees, they waiting. Old men, floppy trousers, scar-tissue skin, they waiting. Younger men, often mumbling to they self, they waiting too.

Buddy leaning on the wall be thinking that the whole city of his people like a all-night emergency room. People mostly suffering, uncomfortable, and waiting.

Police reach the building where Angela live. Find the apartment Buddy describe to them and knock on the door. Does he, Mr. Figueroa, have a daughter name of Angela?

"Yes."

"She home?"

"No."

"Where is she?"

Angela father say he don't know. "She sneak out, din't leave no note."

"Has your daughter done this before?"

"No."

"Anything unusual happen tonight?"

"I tell her show some more respect."

"Where's your wife?"

"Sleeping."

"Don't you want to know what has happened to your daughter, why we're here?"

"No. Maybe one of her boyfriends beat her."

The police demand to talk to Angela mother. They take her back with them to the hospital. Before they leave, Angela mother put on her uniform.

At the hospital, Angela mother approach the stretcher, like a professional.

"Yes, that's Angela."

"Do you know what happened to her?"

"No. Maybe one of her boyfriends beat her."

"She have a boyfriend name Buddy?"

Mrs. Figueroa start to accuse Buddy, but she think of Buddy father, change her mind.

"Mrs. Figueroa, we need you to answer some questions and give permission for the hospital to treat your daughter. She's in serious condition. Will you do that?"

Angela mother shrug her agreement and go into the Administration Office with the police.

The desk attendant keep his eye on Buddy leaning like stone at the back of the Emergency Room. Buddy almost frozen there and barely blink his eyes. The attendant feel sorry for him, and after making some inquiries, he go back and tell Buddy the word:

"Your girlfriend's in shock. They take her to the X-ray. Check out if she have a fracture. She lose a lot of blood, you know."

The attendant keep halting. Expect Buddy to say something. Buddy say nothing, just look away.

"That must have been some terrible beating. You listening to me? Boy, what's the matter?"

Buddy roll his eyes towards the man face, slowly, see a kindly looking guy, brown skin with a clip mustache.

Buddy tell him, "Well, you betta watch your language."

The kindly guy feel better because Buddy have answer him at last.

"Hey, man, why don't you take a load off the floor? Sit down someplace. You not helping nobody standing up there. It's gone be a while."

"Okay."

Buddy move towards a open space, take a seat. Everywhere around him people into pain. Or asthma. Or just plain cold. They using the long wait as a kind of rescue from the street. Buddy thinking and feeling about Angela. Buddy thinking and feeling about his father. The life of the only two people, his father and his girl, inside this hospital.

Buddy jump a little bit. Is he praying?

Buddy don't believe in God, but he catch himself inside his head like he be praying Angela, my father, Angela, my father. Help me. Somebody. Help.

Both the two lives may be dying now, and nothing he can do. Buddy look around him, feel ridiculous, deserted, lonely, sitting there. Consider how much money do he have. Dollar seventy-five. And all at once his pockets swell with cash.

Him, Buddy, up and down the aisle of the Emergency Room.

Ask the lady "want some coffee?" Ask the man "you want a taste?" Pass out chewing gum and Hershey bars and Bali Hai and hot chocolate and hot coffee, lotsa cream. Got the sugar in his hand. Drop the sugar, one lump, two. Pass out pillows, airplane blankets. Taking towels to the men's room, roll up carts of toilet paper, two-ply tissue, soft, oval sweetly scented soap. Strap himself to a outside window belt and wash the windows. Jump down afterwards and rush and grab a broom and sweep and mop, then wring the mop. Bop into his father room. Close the curtains, lower the bed, take a shower, shake his head. Rush out find a florist, buy some flowers, tulips look to him like Angela.

For his father buy some seeds, and haul some open land into the hospital.

Buddy sitting still where he has sat.

seven

They call it child abuse. They mean when Angela get beat so bad the hospital have to treat her.

But why Angela parents have to work so hard and long and why they have to live so crowded up they saying nothing. Point no finger. Take no action. Still the consequences standing pretty terrible and clear. The beating Angela have suffer come through pretty terrible and clear. The Family Court hold Angela in custody. Send Angela to what the Court call "shelter," in Manhattan.

Angela brothers and sister be parcel out among the relatives until police will finish the investigation. When Angela seem well to leave the hospital a large policewoman bring her to the "shelter" in Manhattan. The shelter cross up between a penitentiary and school. Look like a regular old school look like a prison. Shelter girls forbidden to see boys. Buddy measuring the place from outside only. Out across the street from where his Angela be force to stay among too many girls women girls, no men. No boys. Only lonely miserable girls kept lonely.

Buddy starving for the sight of Angela.

The sound of her.

Dictionary tell him shelter keep you safe from danger. He be worrying about a "shelter" separating her from him. He be worrying about old people when they think that love be dangerous.

eight

A couple weeks go by. Buddy father slipping into worse condition. Doctors tell him, anyday. Buddy go to school and blank out in the classroom chair. Thinking and feeling about Angela. Think about her face. Think about how small she seem. Think about her breasts. Think about her room.

In Phys. Ed. Buddy organize his friends. They make it plain they don't want no phony one-two exercising. They want real live physical education: sex education. Want straight films on sex. Want to learn anatomy. Buddy want to know what Angela look like inside. That where the giggle come from. They want contraceptives. They want sex free and healthy like they feel it. Buddy want his Angela.

The principal say no. So Buddy organize his friends. His friends organize their friends. They organize some more. All come together in the gym. Confront the principal.

"What do we want?"
"Sex!"
"When do we want it?"
"Now!"
"What do we want?"
"Sex!"
"When do we want it?"
"Now!"

Principal be very annoy. Principal, a balding son of somebody, send for the A. V. teacher. Ask him bring a tape recorder and a microphone. Buddy and his friends raise the chant:

"What do we want?"
"What do we need?"
"When do we need it?"
"When do we want it?"

The A. V. man arrive carrying a tape recorder and a microphone. The principal trying to bring the gym to order. Fifteen hundred boys calling out:

"Now!"
"Sex!"
"Now!"
"Sex!"

Principal say, "Boys! Boys!"

They lower the chant into a growling consultation among themselves. Come up with a new cry:

"Girls! Girls!"
"Two-four-six-eight-why don't you coeducate?"
"Girls! Girls!"
"Two-four-six-eight-coeducate-coeducate!"
"When do we want it?"
"Now!"

"Wow! Now! Girls! Girls!"

The principal call out: "I am willing to negotiate, send me your leader."

Tremendous roar of laughter break loose from the boys.

They rush forward as one man, Buddy at the front. Present the principal with their demands. Talk back and forth. The principal agree to order films immediately. But he want to negotiate the contraceptives.

The boys appoint a committee who will meet with the principal, settle the details, settle the details. Design a contraceptive clinic. Buddy shove a clipboard underneath the principal nose. Tell him he will write down the particulars of the agreement. Sign it on the spot.

The principal capitulate. Anyway, what can he argue? Do he want more unwed mothers? Tense unhappy students in the classroom? Rape around the corner? Streets too dangerous for his wife to walk down them alone? Mr. Hickey sign the paper.

Buddy handspring somersault high hysterical and happy flying down the lunchroom. Want to eat some food.

He reach the lunchroom. Smell the starchy cheese smell. Slide by the dry steam succotash. The superpeel potato. Stale whole wheat bread. The jerkoff corny butter squares.

Buddy say "God-damn!"

His friend ask, "What you mean?"

Buddy say, "Today. From now. No more. No more eating garbage. And no more this rig-the-lunchroom garbage meaning that we have to squeeze uptight against the walls."

Buddy look around. Tell his lieutenant, "Get the biggest baddest phonograph and get it down here quick." Tell his right-hand man, "Go find some sides. Don't care where you get them. Get them. And bring them here."

Spot the lunchroom supervisor. Give out the word. The boys fall in behind him, close and ready. Buddy move slow to the supervisor Mr. Jenkins. Loudly put his question.

"Mr. Jenkins, why you scrunch up all the tables one side of the lunchroom?"

"Listen here, Rivers. What you trying to do?"

"No, man, answer me. Why we got to sit in all these tables jam up to the side like that?"

Mr. Jenkins reach out to hold on Buddy arm.

"Don't you touch me, Brother Jenkins."

"Rivers, I can explain this to you privately."

"I don't wanna hear no *privately*."

"You can understand, it's a lot easier."

"Don't you tell me what I understand. You tell me what you have to say, then I'll tell *you* what I understand."

"Only two of us patrol the lunchroom, Rivers. You know that." Jenkins talking quickly, nervous now about the boys surrounding him. "Make it easier to control the situation."

"Control!" Buddy mimicking. "Control. You pack us in like animals, and then you say, they

act like nothing more than animals. To hell with
your control." Buddy start to snap his fingers,
rhythmic. Snap. Snap.
   Get it together!
   Snap. Snap. Snap. Snap.
   Get it together.
   Snap. Snap. Snap. Snap.
   Other students pick it up. Snap. Snap. Snap. Snap.
   Get it together.
   Buddy say, "Shit. Must be some women in this
lunchroom. Find the women!"
   Snap. Snap. Snap. Snap.
   Buddy dash. Buddy dash over to the counter.
Jump the counter. Run over, hold a woman.
   "Hey, sweetheart, I know you *got* to be some-
body's mother! Am I right or wrong?"

   The woman try to be angry with him, but she
laugh.
   Buddy say, "Come on, big Momma, dance with
me!"
   Buddy urge the woman out. The other boys be
imitating what he do. Find all them women in
the lunchroom. Bring them out, and proud. Buddy
yell, "Some music, jim, some music!"
   First lieutenant plug the phonograph and wail
the volume to the limit. The music start. The boys
push drag and shove the tables out the way.
Furore in the lunchroom. Big Mommas in the
middle, like church sisters taking care a ceremony.
Dignified, and happy. Rocking to the beat.
   The boys be jumping on the tables. Snatch some

silverware. Beat the furniture to drums. Beat and stamp and clap and dance, and listen to the music. Moving to the music. Making up the music. In the middle, all the Mommas jiggle and they wiggle, dip and strut, break and shake. Take the handkerchief from out the pocket of they uniform. Wipe they forehead. Rock around the floor. Rock. Rock. Rock. Snap, snap. Stamp, stamp. Turn the lunchroom on.

Seven hundred young Black men and four big Mommas doing a dance, in the Boys High lunchroom.

They having so much fun, they hardly hear the sirens racing to the school. The police rush in at the four doors to the lunchroom. Stand there stupefied. Try to figure out what's happening.

Some of the students leap right over, friendly style, ask, "Any women with you?"

Police uncertain what to do. Suddenly the music stop. Mr. Hickey cross the lunchroom, hurriedly on the diagonal. "Arrest him! Arrest him! Where is Rivers? Arrest him!"

The dancing stop.

Buddy come right over to Hickey. Ask him, "Are you looking for me?"

"There he is. Book the troublemaker. Get him out of my school."

Sergeant look around, see all the boys friendly and relax. He see the big Mommas smiling hope to dance some more.

"What's the charge?"

"Disorderly conduct, idiot!"

"Who are you calling 'idiot'? Mr. ——?"

"Hickey. I'm the principal here."

Sergeant look at the floor and say, "Disorderly conduct. You got a printed rule prohibit dancing in the lunchroom, Mr. Hickey?"

"Printed?! You know the rules, Sergeant. You can see for yourself what has happened here!" Exasperated, he shouts, "Jenkins! Where are you?"

Jenkins stroll slowly over to the principal. Jenkins looking at the four big Mommas. Think about his own. He say, "Mr. Hickey, we—"

Hickey interrupt him. "We!?"

"Well, I—I mean—the fellas—you know—and I—just have some music going on. You know, break the monotony, change from the routine."

So the talk goes. The sergeant shake his head and leave the lunchroom, laughing. Ask the Mommas, "How you doing? How's everything?"

They tell him everything be fine.

But Buddy be suspended.

And beside the principal tell Buddy that he can't come back to school unless he bring a parent with him. Buddy think about how dumb the idea is: his parents. Would have to mean a uncle or a aunt come up explaining and polite. Buddy rather wait until his father maybe leave the hospital and come to school: his father be right there to deal with the principal. So Buddy have to stay suspended.

nine

Time and time and day and night Buddy be alone.
At the hospital, he watch his father, hanging on,
unconscious. Live on sugar, flow down from a
bottle through a tube into a vein of his muscular
and idle arm.

Buddy try for small talk with Mrs. Figueroa. But
she give him the glaring of her ugly eye. Angela
be transfer from the shelter to a Catholic Home
for Girls, outside the city, call St. Margaret.

Buddy be practicing to drive his father's car the
long way up to Angela in Middlebrook. He have
been around the local corners some before but
never no long practice drive to get him ready for
the big trip.

Tuesday he decide to practice right around the
city where the traffic bars the river from the people. Buddy off into a territory takes it thirty-five
miles per at midday in-between what folks call
heavy. Thirty-five miles per.

The car run like two tons of filthy thick and deeply spotted oil down Halsey Street between the Blackwood Keep-Your-Neighborhood-Clean placards tilted up strict in the flowerless front yards of redandyellow grayandbrown brownstones. Then the street merge into Fulton Street and subway stops. The workclothes clothingstores. Novelty shops. Goodwill centers. Secondhand refrigerators icebox bedspring coffeepercolator shoes and dresses trouserpants and earmuffs. Fish and barbecue and Jesus Saves Me tabernacles. Drug and beautybarbershops. A stonewhite Virgin Mary statue and a place where Flats Be Fixed and Records Sold at Bargain Prices. Fulton Street.

One time Buddy want to buy a present for Angela so he walk Reid Avenue past all the short thin younger kids who live half in the hallway half on the avenue. Go walk on up to Fulton Street and bop into one shop after another. Find nothing but the smell of old cheese and old fat men with dirty smiles. Or else the smell of old yellow cheese and heavy dust covered crap nobody ever want under Easter egg sloppycolor cellophane.

Nothing good enough for Angela. And you know the price be twice as high as downtown.

Buddy drive down Fulton Street and onto Flatbush Avenue between the blank big office buildings mostly vacant on each side. And then he reach the bridge go over it and cross Canal Street. Make a right turn. Take the West Side Highway north.

The highway like a Funny House. You don't

know when something will open at you let you off or what. Drive north past the storybook apartment houses. People dress up for the movies. Dress down to walk the dog. Drive by below the marble bullshit memory of Prez Grant.

Drive by these Bronxlike Mountainside apartments. Look like highrise outhouse and no door. No tree. Drive across the narrow northern edge of the Manhattan secret-island (people use it like the island part's a secret part). Under a tunnel under eight different intersecting streets under skyscraping (more) apartments on top of George Washington Bridge and curve onto the East Side Drive. The really river drive by Harlem. Brick projects. Brick new private terracing apartments globelights and concrete colored intermix construction bricks. Drive quiet by the river. Harlem bridges start to sway out the windshield.

Drive toward the crowded power down the East Side Drive. And Buddy just be Buddy practicing for the long trip up to Angela.

About the level of 123d Street the Drive spread wider than it was and Buddy tense a bit like a pilot in a mission cockpit.

Check the gauges. Check the rearview mirror. Check the sideview mirror. Watch them cars ahead. The radio be playing loud and nice.

Wrapped up my money
and I couldn't find my way.
So I changed them bills to silver
And I rolled another game

so two could play
so two could pay.
And things ain't never been the same
since then
since when you came
you blew my lonely game with
love like a nickel and a dime
making changes all the time
love like a nickel love like a dime
making changes all the time.

Static. Buddy snap to. The drive be under a stone shed tunnel now. Radio song turn to static. Buddy feel a shivering. He see in the rearview mirror a large black car. A hearse and yellow headlights follow him. And snakestyle behind the hearse more of them. Largedarkcars and yellow lights.

Buddy feel fear.

Not able to switch lanes because there be no room for him. Broad daylight and they in this tunnel and this largedarkcar with yellowlights and other largedarkcars with yellowhearseheadlights be following right after Buddy.

They leave the tunnel to the broad daylight again but still the funeral procession following close right after him and Buddy feel panic.

Why they following after him? Where they going on the Drive? No cemeteries in this direction anywhere. This direction take you to the midtown city center of the power. Where's the cemetery for the funeral behind him? Buddy switch lane.

The largedark car behind him switch lane behind him and the other yellow headhearse-lit large dark cars switch into line following after Buddy.

Him Buddy start to sweat. Another stoneshed tunnel upahead and under it the first hearse pull next to Buddy make Buddy feel like a midget. Look up and see the gargoyle gladioli flowers of the funeral like watercolor swords ready to ram another any corpse around.

Buddy frantic want to separate himself from this funeral procession. Find the next exit and leave the Drive entirely. On the midtown Manhattan sidestreet from the highway Buddy wheel the car to the curb and halt the engine underneath a No Parking Anytime sign. Scared sitting in a small sweat. Buddy don't want to drive no more. Get out and stretch his legs. (Illegal because the sign means on your seat and off your feet.)

From the East River walking west across Forty-ninth Street. Buddy want to cross Second Avenue. He look up north and see the midtown city see the carhorizon taxicolored truckcolored car-colored steel flowers for the funeral. He see the midtown city cemetery and the cold flowers the carsteel flowers filling up the land of stone.

Buddy turn to snatch his car and move it home.

ten

Angela send him a letter:

Dear Buddy,

How are you?

I am fine. I am staying at St. Margaret's in Middlebrook, New York. It's this home for girls again.

How is your father? I hope he is feeling better.

If you want to, you can write me here. They let me get my mail if the letters are all right. The sisters are very nice, and they read my mail before I can read it.

We eat, sleep, and go to school and everything all in the same one building.

If I don't get in trouble, I can have a visitor at the end of the month. Do you think you can come and see me?

Love,

Angela

eleven

Buddy read the letter again and again. Figure the sisters must be censoring the mail, or else Angela be brain damage from when her father hit her in the head. Buddy not sure what to think, but he have hope that it be censorship. End of the month leave him one week to wait until he see her.

He start a garden. Shovel clear some walkway for the garden. Buy cement and mix it with a strong rose coloring for Angela. She will walk around the earth the color of a rose. He pour the cement mix into a S shape in the yard and around it be planting roses and chrysanthemums, a pear tree and some marigold.

Buddy like working in the dirt. He like the feel of soil under the fingernails and mud changing shape in the palm of a hand or the slight chill shiver of a slow moving earthworm.

His relatives, and even sometimes his mother far away in Barbados, they all send him, send Buddy, food money and money for clothes. Treat him like a little man. He take all the clothes money and spend it ordering seeds from a garden catalog his father always use to use, with color photographs of fruit trees and things like that.

The backyard seem like a flower island in the middle of the block. Buddy stare at the fencing separate the people keep every yard too small. Keep every yard a secret angry under the windows. The alley cats the only living action yard to yard.

Then Buddy get himself a plan and go around to make it happen. Buddy want to tear the separating fences down. At first the people tell him when he talk to them they worry that the junkies will rob and steal out stuff from the new back openspace. But Buddy argue how the back be just as hard to enter as the front of houses. So everybody try it.

Pretty soon the neighbors break the backyard open. Pull the fencing down. Stretch the yard into a park they all will share. Have a great big smoky BarBcue to celebrate. Working the ground with neighbors. Planning the backyard park so there be different things that you can use it for. Buddy be less alone and busy. They have a huge dump of sand somebody bring in and even the older kids spread into it. Have a ball. The men plan how to share the hose they have for waterplay when summer start.

Things looking up. People on the block say hello and talk awhile.

Buddy spend all the money he hold on work stuff, seed, tools, paint. He be losing weight.

He write to Angela:

Last night it rain, and I go walking out. I notice how the sidewalk looks blue when it rain. So I buy some strong blue paint to paint the sidewalk strong blue all the time. Then a taxi fly by and I been thinking about your father and I look at the steps lead to the parlor. They probably look better black and yellow. Done that today. Then I buy some slick gray paint to trim the windows. I would like to paint the street a bloody red where cars go through.

But the people on the block don't really dig all this painting that I do. They come around complaining. Yak. Yak.

Tell me what they feed you. Good cooking is hard to come by. Do you know how? To cook?

See you soon.

Buddy

Dear Angela:

I be the first one there on Saturday, see for myself what's happening to you.

Yesterday I make this table. Be like the Japanese. The table seem like a triangle. One point be the food and the other points be for you and me. It stand 15 inches high, from off the floor. Like I said, you can call me Slim. I hope you slim the same. Otherwise, it be uncomfortable.

Stain it what they call a rosewood coloring. I got this thing for roses, and for you. When the table be finish, I put it next to the big floor pillows where *you* can lie down listen to the phonograph, which I still ain't finish put together, but I have in mind because of you.

Love,
Buddy

twelve

Saturday arrive. Buddy driving up to Angela. Drive by houses, drive by parkside, drive by gasoline station, drive by the state police, drive by highway over the highway, drive by byways by the highway, drive by other people, other cars, traveling in the same, the opposite direction. Cross across them. Drive by boats. Drive by pond and river. Drive by train and railroad track.

Take a long time getting there.
Angela see Buddy and her heart beat hard.
She say, "You looking skinny."
He say, "You watch out. You be like a heavyweight."
"Sister Frances, this is Buddy Rivers."
"How you, Sister?"
Buddy see the sister trying to hide her face from the light. Seem like she shave her face.

"Sister Mary this my friend, Buddy Rivers."

"How you, Sister Mary?"

Buddy notice Sister Mary look like a football fullback off the field.

"Sister Margaret, this be Buddy Rivers. He my friend from Brooklyn."

Buddy think she look all right and wonder why the Sister Margaret be a nun.

Angela introduce Buddy to every single sister this and that. Buddy think the bunch of them be like some fallen angels. Fallen out of life.

"Ain no priests up here, Angela?"

"Why you asking me?"

"The sisters need some boyfriends. Something make them act alive. I come up and be a altar boy! Get this heavy incense. Throw it all around the chapel. Everybody be high."

"Buddy, stop that."

"Stop what? How you like it up here, nothing but the sisters and the girls?"

"Let's go where we can really talk."

"Where's that?"

"You have to go outside. No place inside where you can be alone. Even for a minute. Even in my room I have four other girls in there with me. Everybody have the same deal. Five to a room."

They go outside. Buddy feel like a fool to ask in case they have a rule against his holding her hand. But he don't want to get his Angela in trouble. So they move out separated stiff.

Angela continue. Almost whisper in a hurry.

"Last week one of them attack me."

"One of who? The sisters?"

"No, not yet. But I hear about a sister on the third floor try to kiss another sister."

Buddy say, "Try to kiss her?" He start to laughing. "Angela you better be serious."

"I am serious," she say, laughing. "Half the girls be going with the other half. They don't let you do nothing else."

"Jesus K. Christ, what you be doing?"

"Well, I write my letters to you, you know. But they be no boys up here and we can't see none except once a month, if we be good. One of my friends, she ask the sister can they pray for all the people who in love. The sister say that's no kind of prayer for anybody in a chapel."

"Dig that."

"And another friend of mine. She suppose to get out when her birthday come. But the sister tell her she have to stay here unless she write her boyfriend and break up with him."

"Why?"

"The sister say they be too serious."

"Damn. What they think Jesus was into?"

"Well I don't know what they think. Except it seem like they want us to turn into nuns like them. Buddy, I don't want to be no nun."

"Why you even have to say that Angela."

Angela don't answer right away. Buddy waiting for the answer. Look at her face and feel himself not strong enough to help.

Angela go on. "They have this system. Points.

More times you go to Mass the more points you be collecting. Points mean you get privileges. Like boys once a month. Or going home for a weekend. So you try for points. Next thing you know you start feeling like already you a nun. I'm fourteen and I think about what be happening when I grow up. Do I want to be like my mother. Do I want to be a nun. And I don't know between my mother and a nun. I don't know no more."

Angela sound funny. Hoarse. Buddy feel scare that she will cry.

"Angela! I break you outa here!"

"What you mean? What you saying?"

"Listen baby, I mean liberation. Here and now! All you gotta do is follow me!"

Tears come from Angela.

And Buddy feel himself whirl around and run back to the building.

Angela running after him.

Buddy bolting room by room trying to find a signal.

Find the dining room bell. And ring the bell and ring the bell and ring the bell. All the sisters run to the parlor look like overheated penguins.

All the girls run to the parlor, look like children.

Buddy ring the bell like bells be going outa style.

Bell, bell, bell.

He make a speech: "In the name of the Father, in the name of the Son, in the name of the Mother who got together with the Father and

got that Son, I liberate my Angela, here and now.
This is Eastertime in Middlebrook. Love is rising
up. Love is rising up. I tell you, Jesus was a one
hundred percent, hip to the living, female-loving
dude. A loving dude."

Buddy make his speech, the nuns come flying
at him. Gray robes, black and shapeless clouds
of cloth material.

Buddy dodge among the nuns, and cry out,
"Peace, peace, sister. Find yourself a priest."

Everything be all confuse, the sisters grabbing
at each other, wide sleeves flapping furious, head-
piece falling off.

The girls thrash to the doorway. Sisters like
obstacles to impede and block their passage. The
girls in sweaters, sisters in robes. Buddy yelling,
"Peace, find yourself a priest."

Buddy grab Angela and tackle through three
sisters, their weight bewildering their movements.
Buddy say, "Sing, Angela, you be singing. This is
liberation!" Angela not say nothing, stay close behind Buddy. Reach the doorsill. Start they running
out to the car. Get inside, discover other girls be
hiding in the car, waiting for the lift, waiting for
liberation.

Buddy start the car, the car take off, they on
they way. And speeding.

Tears continue from her eyes and Buddy standing still in front of Angela. Hands at his side.

Angela say, "Buddy, next weekend they let me

go home. Visit my family for the weekend. Buddy. You want me to come to you then?"

Buddy answer her *yes*. His head feel hot. His eyes feel hot. His body cold. They plan together what will happen. When she leave her parents Sunday for the trip back up to Middlebrook. Then instead she will come to the house of Buddy and his father. Then they will then they will then they will do what they have to do. For liberation.

thirteen

Buddy believing that alive mean *go*. He do it. He go there. Do this. Do that. Not so much the speed, but the pattern. Do it. Go there. Make a pattern. Break a pattern. Back and forwards, round and round. Curve and drift. Stop to start. Start to stop. Blur and solid:

> When I'm alone with you
> All my worries taking flight
> All my sadness out of sight
> When I'm alone with you
> When I'm alone with you
> When I'm alone
> With you alone.

Buddy trying to prepare for love inside the house of his father. He nail together and he sand things smooth. Clean and clear. Write down write up long list of things he wish that he could spread

around for Angela to see. Then he sit down quiet
thinking songs and thinking of his father. Think-
how they Angela and Buddy have to find a way
to stay together.

Angela come back to Brooklyn with a paper bag.
When she reach the building where her family
live she feel a freezing terror. But she go inside.
Her brothers and her sister have been sent away
and so the house seem hopeless ugly.

Angela sit down in the parlor on the couch. She
waiting for her mother or her father when he will
get off from working.

She check the refrigerator. Find no food. No
stuff for snacking. One piece of meat be frozen
rocky. Bread seem rocky. Milk smell sour. Only
thing available is beer. A couple six-packs and a
saucer holding gray beans leftover.

On the stove, a big pot bubbling steady full of
peas and hambone.

"Angela! What you doing here?"

Her mother shut the front door and immediately
call out.

"Hello, Ma." Angela leave the kitchen and walk
into the parlor where her mother have snap on
one of the big lamps no one hardly use.

"They kick you out, or what?"

"I'm just visiting for the weekend."

"Visiting! Hah. Freeloading be closer to the
truth. They give you money? or do you expect
that we will feed you for free?"

Angela want to sit down and be deaf. Be dumb. Be blind. She have no heart to argue with her mother. She miss her brothers and her sister. Now she realize she have no home. Her family be parents beat you in the head or hate you. She mean the father mother family. Her sister and her brothers make another family where she love and care. Angela trying to think how she can come around the hatred of her mother. How she can have a home that be a happy place be better than the upstate "home" for girls.

"Well, Miss Angela, you have in mind to sit on your behind and watch me slave a little bit?"

"Oh, Ma. Look, if you want me to do something tell me straight."

"Now you criticize the way I talk?"

"I only mean why we have to fight? Tell me what you want me to be doing. Period. I'll do it."

"If you so smart about the way I should be talking you don't need me to tell you nothing at all. For all I care you can go on and sit there, or stand upside down. I'm going out."

"Ma, you want me to go back upstate?"

"You got yourself into that mess."

"Ma, Daddy put me in the hospital. He beat me."

"I don't care what you do but do it out my sight. Don't let me hear you say no words about your father."

"Ma, I be going back upstate tonight. Right now."

"Well, what you waiting for? You see anybody stop you?"

Angela look at her mother long. She look around the room. Small room. Big empty dust feeling to the furniture. Dust.

Angela pick up the paper bag. Finally she take the housekey from her pocket. Put it on the television. "Okay, Ma, I'm going now," she say. And Angela go. She leave for good.

fourteen

Angela hope Buddy be home. They have plan for Sunday. But the day is now. Friday.

She walk the avenue toward the subway and his house. Somebody come up from behind and hug around her close and large.

"Hey, where you going Angela?"

"See you." She turn around and into Buddy arms. Repeat. "See you."

They quick discuss the scene. They figure that tonight be safe enough. The nuns think Angela be visiting her parents and her parents think that Angela be traveling back to Middlebrook. Things seem temporary cool. Both Buddy and Angela feel excited trembling almost almost ready for the liberation they have scheme together.

"You have any money?"

Buddy nod his head.

"Maybe we should pick some food up."

"Okay. Let's go buy some bananas, some potato chips, some ice cream, and some soda. What you want?"

"I like a hamburger, some tissues and some soap."

"You need any of them—ah, what you may call female things?"

"If I do, I get them on my own time, Mr. Rivers!"

"Don't say I didn't ask you!"

"Angela, what you think about this store?"

Got burglar gates and great big locks. You can't hardly go inside the place. Place be halfway burn. Ashes on the floor.

"Look like a jail where food be taken out on bail."

Angela answer nothing.

Inside the store, they nudge each other when they see a roach slip by. Buy what they want. Buddy crumple up his dollar bills before he turn them over to the man.

"Don't be right to give them something green and pretty."

They run back to Buddy block.

"Come on, come on, let's get inside! We got one night."

Angela start laughing when she see the steps. Black and yellow just like Buddy wrote. They take them two at a time, two at a time.

First thing Angela notice when she step in the

door, she smell sawdust, airplane glue and paint. Angela just standing by the door, make her eyes roam around the house.

Her eyes be roaming around the house.

The house very surprising. From the street it look like a three-floor brownstone. The outside stone steps take you to the front door, and that front door take you inside. And then, the big surprising part of the house begin because you see no hallway. No hallway. There be indoor stairs lead to a third floor. The indoor stairs be part of the living room on the second floor where you be standing inside the house.

The third floor be like a balcony, tore back from the downstairs living room and overlook that living room.

Most of the living room reach from the second floor, where you standing, to the roof. And, in a funny place, not really in the center of the ceiling of the roof, there be a stain-glass skylight, blue and red and purple and plain light, high up in the ceiling/roof of the living room.

So the house seem huge inside it. Huge and high. With the stairways zigzag on the side. Some of the steps unstained, unpainted. Maybe two piece of furniture in the living room. A easy chair. A portable TV.

Planks of lumber lean against the walls, and one window almost floor to ceiling, with a brand-new sticker on the corner of it. The other window be broken brick by brick. And temporary cardboard block the air until the wall will hold a longer pane of glass.

The wall be plaster rough. Some paper stripping curl toward the floor, and other parts be painted blue already.

Angela feel like she walking in a magazine before the final photograph be taken of the house. Before everything be finish.

No hallway. Angela stare hard to see a house where people live without a hallway. That mean every part of the house is real. It belong to somebody, and be part of how you live, not how you get to where you live, and be.

Buddy calling "Come on, Sister Angela." Buddy pound down the stairs, drop the package, and pound back up. "See how much weight you gain."

Buddy lift her to his shoulder, tell her, "Hold on."

Buddy walking tiptoe tremble, make believe the weight will kill him. Start to groaning. Groan all the way down the stairs, out to the garden, where he stand her up.

"Let me watch you walking on the concrete. How you like it?"

Angela see flowers not yet blooming any color. See the narrow pretty strip of path. A strong rose concrete way among the growing flowers. See the mud, the warm rich earth, a natural brown.

"Walk with me, Buddy."

"Not enough room, Angela."

"How can you make something so narrow, there be no room for two of us?"

"I guess I didn't think you come here, really."

"Dance with me, Buddy, then we can fit it."

Buddy move to Angela move to Buddy, like one person, moving on the concrete running red through the brown earth.

"They be some hard buttons on your coat."

"Well, I'm allergic to the wool you wearing. How you like it?"

"Here is really nice. I really like it."

"You want a soda?"

"I like a soda, but I like to wash my hands and wash my face, and then I like to come back out here."

"It be dark soon, Angela, we can come back out here, maybe later."

Buddy think about tomorrow. But don't even want to *say* tomorrow.

"Buddy, where the bathroom? I never see a house like this."

Buddy bend down to the floor, hold a knob there. When he come up, part of the wall come up with him. "There you go."

"Why you have a door like that?"

"Be good exercise, bend down, pull up, bend down, open it up. You get use to it. Everything in this house be like this."

She go in the bathroom. Whole room like the doorway to it. Seem like wood venetian blinds.

Dark wood strips look like they comb down smooth, or almost smooth together, like venetian blinds. The soap, the shower curtain, bathtub mat, the towel and the washcloth, the toothbrush and the box of baby powder, everything except the mirror and the walls, be crazy orange. Angela uneasy. Real quick wash her hands and face with orange soap, and dry her hands and face on orange towels, smelling clean and good.

"Buddy, something happen to me! You better come on in, and see!"

Buddy calling, "What you doin?"

"My face turn orange in the bathroom. That be some really sneaky soap."

Buddy lift up the door, go inside look at Angela. Her face seem orange in the mirror. She look at him.

"You have the same disease."

Buddy step behind her, bring his face down to her face. They see each other in the mirror, orange.

"You better let me see how bad it is. It may be spreading."

"You always try to be so smart."

Buddy say, "Square business. It look serious to me. Better check it out."

He look close to her neck. Buddy say, "Oh, oh— you can see for yourself, you got a bad case of the orange."

Angela turn from the mirror, start to tickling him.

"Hey, woman, I'm a break my neck."

Buddy try to escape the tickling, bang his elbow

on the sink, knock his head against the towel rack. Buddy say "shh . . . ."

Whip off the light. Whisper, "Here, hold on to this." Give Angela a piece of towel. "Don't make no noise, just hold on to the towel."

Buddy pull Angela slowly, quietly out the bathroom to the dining room—what use to be dining room. Buddy give Angela all the towel. He say, "Here, hold this on your eyes."

Press the lightswitch, make like a purple light on everything. "Okay. You can look now. Here, come here. You choose a record."

Buddy lift up the phonograph cabinet door and, smiling, show his Angela the phonograph, the albums pile together, thick. The room not finish yet, but almost.

One corner there the wires hang down from the ceiling, and no light. Toolbox and some tools beneath the music cabinet.

"Let me take your coat."

Buddy put the coats inside a large wood box built like a trunk against the wall. He lift the lid and fold the coats and pack them out of sight.

The music be the only sound. He dancing with her, slow enough to hear her breathe.

She say, "I wish we could just stay here."

"We can. A little while. Tonight."

They sit down on the mattress in the corner, flat against the floor.

"You think we get in trouble, Buddy?"

"I don't know. I'm glad you're here."

They be quiet holding close together. He kiss her mouth, her arm.

Her fingers teasing on his neck and trace the fire down his back, his back a bone and skin discovery she making, stroke by stroke.

And they undress themselves. Feel him feel her wet and lose the loneliness the words between them.

"What do you call it?" Buddy ask her.

"Well I call it making love."

"We make some love."

They make some love and then they fall asleep.

fifteen

Next morning they legs be tangle together. Angela wake up and look at Buddy lying naked there beside her. She kiss Buddy face, lean on one elbow looking at his head.

Buddy waken. He turn over, rest her warm against his chest. "Angela, I thought you was a virgin. But maybe you should of told me that you was a virgin. I mean I'm sorry. Are you all right?"

Angela say, "For real. It dint hurt no more after that one time I told you."

Buddy smiling say, "I'm glad you all right."

Angela laughing. "Well, you all right too, Buddy."

Suddenly Buddy sit up, exclaim, "You could be pregnant!" Turn around and hug her hard. "Hey, you know that one thing? Could be we have a baby coming soon!"

Angela answer him by saying, "That be fine with me. So long we be both together, taking care of business."

"Well, of course," he say excited. "Start with two of us, and go right on ahead, the two of us be taking care of three of us."

"What time is it?"

"Time we better move on outa here. Sometime soon the sisters *and* the police *and* your parents figure things through and we be trapped by them."

"Well, let's eat some bananas and some ice cream and then you tell me what we need to take so I can help you pack."

Buddy tell her while they dress themselves. They take the food, the toolbox, a saw, his portable radio, extra batteries, some soap and towels, can-opener, kaleidoscope, playing cards, picnic jug of water, all the blankets they can find, two pillows, paper, ballpoint pens, drafting supplies for Buddy to fool with, flashlight, candles, and matches.

They quickly load the car and slowly lock the house.

Get to the corner. Make two left turns. Drive down the street where you can still see iron trolley tracks from years ago. Drive from the neighborhood they know. Make a right turn put them on Bushwick Avenue. Look out for cops. Take the road into the cemetery. Leads them to the reservoir brick house.

Just before they reach the house they see a military burial ground. Seem like all them same white crosses turning death to boredom. White crosses. Here and there a dime-store flagstick. Eight inches high, stuck into the earth. Its small flag leaking slight and lonely color to the lonely formal ground.

Buddy say, "A flag is not a flower growing on you. When I die, I want something to grow on right on top of me, you know?"

Angela be silent. She don't want to think about the end of nothing. Everything just really starting up.

When he stop the car, Buddy raise the hood, pretend he fooling with the radiator, and Angela act swift. Make several fast trips to unload the car on the side away from the highway eyes, the side of the reservoir house where she will wait for Buddy.

He drive the car two miles farther on, take off the tags, and hike back to where she waiting.

Angela sit among the things sad and scared. She listen to the traffic while she hypnotize herself by studying the sunlight in the water.

Finally Buddy come back like a silhouette approaching her. He kiss her forehead and then swamp her with blankets wrap around her. Leave her looking like a tepee.

Buddy take a hammer and a wedge. Break into the house. Look around. Break up the cobwebs. Saw some, drill some openings into the boards that covering the windows. Let in some air and light.

Must be a toolshed people have forgot about. Buddy rake the floor to clear it. Find a spigot, fill a pail with soap and water. Slosh the floor to weight the dust down. Make things smell better.

When he go out until the floor will dry, he find that Angela have scale the fence and be halfway in the water.

"Angela! The cars be seeing you that way!"

She laugh at him, and after a while, come back.

"We stay here long enough, we could figure how to swim here safe without nobody seeing us. Like at night. But now you never know."

"They don't have no guards around here?"

"I never seen one. Come on inside and dig the house."

"Hey, so much stuff! So much equipment, this is really outasight. You probably knew you could work it out, didn't you? Can you use them things some way?"

"First thing I need to do is find some wood. And maybe buy some glass and screens. Then I could show you better."

They talk to keep the house around them. His voice her voice shape him and her familiar (shapes) inside the unfamiliar house. They talk but standing still talk trying to imagine how they can stay and move and sleep and change where they are standing now, inside.

"We have enough money for about two weeks. If we find a store nearby, we can take turns going so they don't know that we together."

"I want everyone to know. Oh, shit, to hell with it. To hell with it. With everyone. I wish we had a rug, right here."

Buddy recognize that Angela be just as scare as

him, and worrying. He think about what to say.

"We can use a blanket, baby. Put a blanket down. Let's try it."

"Buddy, open up the door so we can see the reservoir and count the birds and watch for the police."

Use up a hour spreading things out comfortable. Then notice that the blanket they been walking on be mess up from the shoes. So they make a rule. Like Orientals they will leave they shoes outside the house. They will leave the outside mess outside. They lay another blanket down, a clean blanket, down on the floor for Angela.

After that they go outside to work together. Shovel a latrine. Make up a bathroom in the bushes at the bottom of the hill.

For a bed, Buddy bang two benches together that he find. Angela figuring that things will be all right. They will eat out of cans and use the water from the spigot. So they settle in.

"I hope they don't be no rats around here. Buddy, why you frowning up like that?"

"I worry about my father. How he is. Don't want him dying by himself alone. Don't want him dying. I worry about myself, I may be a father soon myself, depending on you, and I worry what we doing here. How long can we hold out?"

"You think your father, you think he will die, Buddy?"

"I don't know what I think. You realize how long it's been since I hear him speak to me, or tell me anything? He don't even know you. Never even seen you, Angela, you. Sometime I think how I will like to give him to you—give you to him. You two meeting, eating oranges or peaches. Can you picture that?"

"I can taste it happening, sometime I think maybe your father would adopt me."

"Listen, Angela, don't start no sister business here with me."

"Okay, Mr. Rivers." They wrestling each other, ticklefighting on the floor.

"If my father was me, he probably take a pencil and scheme some changes for the house."

"Why don't you do that?"

"If I do, what will you be doing?"

"Oh, I play the radio. Figure something out I have in mind."

First thing Buddy draw is trees. He have the tree between the highway and the house. But still, you know, the highway is there, the house is there, and now you have the trees. Nothing cut into nothing else. But things be differently together. From the highway, things seem different. From the house, the road seem different. But no interference. No elimination. No taking out the highway or the house. The trees be added on, be something more. And the same be better with the trees.

Next he mark in some plants, some vegetables, and some flowers. Then he have the whole roadside of the house be brick completely. Except for near the bottom where he draw a wall-to-wall long narrow window as wide as the house is wide. So when he and Angela lie down they can see outside but not be seen unless somebody crawl up on his stomach.

On the reservoir waterside the house be absolutely glass with blinds for when they need them. And then there be a fireplace. Buddy not sure about how practical really is a fireplace, and so instead he draw a big potbelly stove, then he scratch that out. Then he try a radiator. Then he scratch out the radiator and then he go back to drawing in the fireplace.

Part of the time, Angela watch. Finally, out loud, she say, "No furniture in that house."

"See, I think a house, a home should mean like the table and the chairs. You build them in. Build in the table like the floor, the doors, the window, and the wall. That way, nothing really loose. Everything is tight, and you can trust it."

"I feel pretty loose, right now. You trust me?"

"I like you better than some table and a chair."

"But you can't nail me down."

"Don't want nobody nail nobody down. I'm only talking about furniture. People move keep moving all around. That be interesting. But let them things stay quiet. Things stay in they place. The same place all the time."

"What you have against people if they sit tight and have like the telephone to do the traveling."

"Well, look, I don't mind the telephone except it be like television and the whole world is a

box-up make-believe to make you think you into
what be really happening but all the time you into
nothing really but that box. I have this other plan."

"Hey, this other plan better be something we
can eat. Plus something we can drink. I choose you
who will go for soda."

Buddy taking odds and lose on the third show,
to Angela. While he go away, Angela comb out her
Afro, fool with the radio, and make some notes.

> Wine grow ready on the vine
> My baby write me letters on his hand
> Night bring the river and the seed
> Love is all the land we need
>
> The wine grow ready on the vine

sixteen

Come back to tuna fish and root beer. Eat and drink away the hunger and the worry.

"What you think," Angela ask Buddy, "Suppose everybody hold a radio. And you already dig how many kinds of sound you maybe hear that way. Depending how you feel, where you be going to, or where you come from, or what you feel like doing."

Buddy close and folding Angela inside his arms to rock with her. They swaying slow.

"I know what I feel like doing."

"Turn it on the radio."

"Damn, Angela."

"Do it, Buddy, please?"

"It? What you mean."

"Find the music on the radio. The music for what you feel."

Buddy take the radio. He turn and turn until he

find a solo horn and strings, a strong drum under them.

They make some love. Buddy drop into a dreaming. Leave his large hands like protection and support around the brown surprising sturdy breasts of Angela.

The Dream

Start on uptown Fulton Street around three o'clock and the streets suddenly be full of children suddenly free from school and crowds and throngs of blackbrown yellow redskin children wearing white shirts/blueskirt uniforms/armysurplus/leftover cousinspringcoats. Crowds and crowds from seven years old up to seventeen. Into every attitude and face. Into every natural style and pace of fights and chase and rap and argument. A hundred and a hundred and ten thousand blackbrown yellow redskin kids suddenly spill into the streets suddenly fill the streets suddenly free from school.

Buddy father be walking the other way alone. His arm around a brown bag of groceries and Buddy father walking careful not to hurt the hundred thousand kids swarm at him surging in the opposite direction thick to circle by the stranger man his groceries. The darkbrown muscle of his motion.

The dream continue around five o'clock on midtown Forty-ninth Street/Fifth Avenue and suddenly them neighborhoods be full of hundreds and ten thousands hundreds of white folks suddenly leaving the towers suddenly leaving floor to ceiling windowwalls walltowall carpets cafeterias lounge areas bigbathrooms easychairs desks sofabed and couch great conference tables heavy leather books addingmachines typewriters desks magazines furnaces that work hot water air conditioning sculpture fountains and 43,785,619 suddenly empty rooms with doors and locks and keys.

Buddy father walking the other way alone up the subway stairs. The thousand other people pushing down (the stairs) Buddy father walking careful not to let himself be hurt. The hundreds rush against around him on his arrival for the night and they be leaving.

The dream continue around midnight, and the empty towers echo harsh from emptiness. Other people women wash the office floors, dust, straighten things. Other men sweep the corridors and rearrange the furniture and distribute a next day supply of comfortable items. Buddy father laugh among these other few men and other few women friends spending the night with him in the otherwise empty towers where he watchman of the night.

The dream continue around dawn and Buddy father working at his pocket drawing pad. Buddy father the nightwatchman at the top on the terrace roof of an otherwise empty skyscraper and now Buddy father draw the inside of the building that he guard and fill the empty tower full of people that he know.

The people and the family of the men and women who do clean and straighten up the towers for the other (morning) folk.

The children from the Brooklyn streets. The relatives of cleaning people Brooklyn children fill his father drawing of the empty towers now a skyscraper glowing full of life at night and through the night.

The dream continue bright from Buddy father drawing pad into another dream and all the crowded, cold, the peeling painted rickety and rusted the unlit shamble Brooklyn housing slide invisible into the Hudson River slide collapsing from a river pier of several thousand splinters. Meanwhile all the families all the Brooklyn people reach the evening empty towers and fill them up with cribs and toys and parties on the intercom and blankets on the leather couch and turnip greens cook steaming in the cafeteria.

Buddy wake from his dream kiss sleeping Angela and she wake up.

He try to talk about his dream but some of it run disappearing from his mind. Buddy tell his Angela about the high-rent houses of apartments and the vacancies, about the Empire State Building and the vacancies, the space no human being use, the cityspace for life where there be emptiness. He try to tell his Angela about the city emptiness at five o'clock, the waste, the rooms no body use at night.

So Angela ask Buddy what he think would really happen if the Brooklyn people use the emptiness, take over space no body else will use inside the city, inside the tower buildings.

Buddy say, "Well, we could share them office buildings. I mean it's pretty wild, you stop to think about it, all them office building empty more than all night long, and all them rich apartments in them rich apartment houses, empty, and the other terrible small houses fall apart, burn up, burn down, and babies dying sick, cold, or sleeping in a orange crate. Don't make no sense."

"But suppose the office folk don't want nobody in they buildings after five."

"Then they could stay up where they living anyhow and do your thing about the telephone. I mean they just use machines, just put them up in the garage, or something, and don't have to use no office in the city. Or, you know what? We could compromise. At first, just use the office that nobody renting anyhow."

"I like it, Buddy. But how you think the businessmen be sharing in the daytime with the folks from Brooklyn?"

"They learn. Even business people, they can learn. From the get-go Brooklyn folks know how to share. They teach them other people nice."

"Buddy, you some heavy dreaming head."

"No. You be the only dream around here, Angela. The only dream."

seventeen

Buddy and Angela lying quiet.

Listen to the traffic 50 mph. The afternoon turn twilight. They decide to bathe each other clean. Too cold to strip completely so they wash each other one part at a time. Pouring water in the big sink drainaway. His legs. The fingers of her hands. And then they trade on washing hair. Her laughing screams. His laughing howl. The icy water shrink the Afros to a brilliant squeaky tangling of black hair.

Go out and wander by the reservoir. Disturb the pigeons. Breathe in the early grass. The highway gasoline. Feel strong. Feel clean. Go out and wander.

When they think about the new house that they leave behind them it seem small almost impossible so small and unpredictable. Not really safe.

Buddy say he miss the lot of people on the

corners out the windows. How they living now by hiding out he miss the action of the people streets and subways and the bus.

He have been at home and out of school and Angela have been away and out of town so long they sure now that the best part of the city is the people mingle bump and spin together various.

Angela say nothing. Walk beside him quiet. Near to evening no one near enough to hear them.

"Angela, you lonely?"

He hold Angela around her shoulder. She slightly leaning on his side. They walking on.

Buddy stop.

"You come on with me. We take some flowers from a grave we find, and bring them back and plant them by the house, right here, tonight."

"I feel spooky doing that."

"We the only spooks out here. I hope."

"Suppose somebody catch us."

"Somebody catch us, you and me, you think they think about some flowers we have borrow from a grave? Last thing people think about is flowers. And if they be after us, they not after no flowers, Angela, stolen or otherwise. Listen, tomorrow we should borrow trees! Trees. Evergreen stuff. Take it to the concrete. Stand it on a stoop. Borrow trees tomorrow."

Buddy run and snatch a branch and swinging on a tree.

Angela run and catch him hold him tight around his ankles.

"Hey, let go!"

Angela let go and flying wild among the cemetery stones. Buddy after her.

They body dodge the headstones.

Running free.

Out of breath they slow and start to search for flowers they could carry back with them and plant again outside the house.

Buddy have to use a flashlight. Mostly finding imitation this and that in plastic. Or else they finding dead plants left to shrivel in the graveyard.

Angela whisper urgent: "Wait, Buddy. Over here. What's that?"

They see some moss in the moonlight look like old tinsel lying down. Look like a growing snowflake. Buddy loosen the earth under and around the patch and then he lift two handfuls clinging soil.

Now Angela shine the flashlight careful so they quickly reach the reservoir and then the house and plant the small green moss almost invisible beside the doorway.

The benchbed seem too hard. They try to sleep together huddling in the highway house.

Well I never come home
my love sing love and the
oversea sky
I never come home.

Well I know I'm not ready to die
my heart like the wind
want to roam
I know I'm not ready to die.

They try to sleep in the house. They give it up
and go out to the ground.

You be different from the dead. All them tomb-
stones tearing up the ground, look like a little
city, like a small Manhattan, not exactly. Here is
not the same.

Here, you be bigger than the buildings, bigger
than the little city. You be really different from the
rest, the resting other ones.

Moved in his arms, she make him feel like smiling. Him, his head an Afro-bush spread free beside
the stones, headstones thinning in the heavy air.
Him, a ready father, public lover, privately alone
with her, with Angela, a half an hour walk from
the hallway where they start out to hold themselves together in the noisy darkness, kissing,
kissed him, kissed her, kissing.

Cemetery let them lie there belly close, their
shoulders now undressed down to the color of the
heat they feel, in lying close, their legs a strong
disturbing of the dust. His own where, own place
for loving made for making love, the cemetery
where nobody guard the dead.

His mouth warm on her lips. They wrap up together shivering strong and tired. Angela dream.

DREAM

See suddenly different neighborhoods.
The city split by sound.
Jazz sound territory. Blues. Country and Western turf.
   Supermarket Muzak. Heavy classical and not so heavy not so classical. And the hospital. A silent zone.
   All the people be like Angela who hold a radio. Use it like a compass on a music map. Tune the dial to what you want. Some hard rock coming very soft. You go the right direction then the sound grow louder on the radio.
   If you don't, it don't. When the sound reach very loud you be along with all those other folk who want to hear the same sound at the same time. In a park. A office building. A ocean liner.
   You never know where you will end up or who you maybe meet there where you going.

   Could be like calypso. Buddy dancing on the way.
   Call out. Is it louder? Is it louder? Maybe thirty thousand people in the street with Buddy dancing on the way. And everybody have a radio. That make a big fantastic street sound by itself.
   People laugh and talk. Men help young Mommas cross the street. Lift up they strollers. Be like a protest marching only now the people getting into music. Really moving into it.

One time on a Sunday she and Buddy follow along to the entrance to the Zoo. There be these twelve-year-olds have put together a steel wash-tub/broomstick group and everyone stay listening and dance. Another time she and Buddy finish up on Fulton Street. All the trucks be detour. And Sparrow and the Duke of Iron real professionals play in the open air. A superparty.

And for some silence there be stations on the radio like a seashell on your ear. Sound like the wind can blow away your mind.

A whistle windsound.

People follow it. Be like a Sunday service. Everybody whisper. Put they fingers to they lips. Follow the silence into someplace like a hospital, a church, a beach, a rooftop, a playground. People like a Quaker meeting silent several hundred silent standing or for example in a library some sit and read or write some meditate.

Or on the grass like a seashell of silence the thousands standing and sit there.

The Last Page

Morning and they do not move.

Arms around and head and cheek the skin and temperature of touch. Buddy hold his Angela but closer now and near enough to hear her breathing regular. Here is how they feel a happiness. Angela awaken looking to his open eyes.

"I hope I'm pregnant, Buddy."

"Hey, Angela. We make that sure enough. And soon."

And so begins a new day of the new life in the cemetery.

about the author

June Jordan was born in Harlem and grew up in the Bedford-Stuyvesant section of Brooklyn—the scene of her first novel, HIS OWN WHERE. She studied at Barnard College and at the University of Chicago, and she has taught at the City College of New York, Connecticut College, and Sarah Lawrence College. She is a cofounder of a creative writing workshop for Black and Puerto Rican teen-agers in Brooklyn. A collection of her own poetry has been published, and she is the editor of two anthologies of Afro-American poetry. The recipient of a Rockefeller Foundation fellowship in creative writing and of the Prix de Rome in environmental design, Miss Jordan is now involved in filmmaking, along with her work as poet and writer.